Magic Pony

Snow Bandits

"GET OUT OF MY WAY!" Penelope yelled at the top of her voice. The boys backed off fast, but Smudger was too late. The barrow clipped his front wheel and he and the bike toppled to the ground. The wheelbarrow reared up – whether helped by Penelope or not, Natty didn't know – and the whole load of manure slid out on top of him.

Follow all of Natty and Ned's
adventures! Collect all the fantastic books
in the Magic Pony series:

Magic Pony

Snow Bandits

Elizabeth Lindsay

Illustrated by Peter Kavanagh

SCHOLASTIC

For Antonia and Bella

Scholastic Children's Books
An imprint of Scholastic Ltd
Euston House, 24 Eversholt Street
London, NW1 1DB, UK
Registered office: Westfield Road, Southam, Warwickshire, CV47 0RA
SCHOLASTIC and associated logos are trademarks and/or registered
trademarks of Scholastic Inc.

First published in the UK by Scholastic Inc, 1999
This edition published in the UK by Scholastic Ltd, 2009

Text copyright © Elizabeth Lindsay, 1999
Illustrations copyright © Peter Kavanagh, 1999
The right of Elizabeth Lindsay and Peter Kavanagh to be identified as the
author and illustrator of this work has been asserted by them.

Cover illustration © Charlotte Macrae

ISBN 978 1407 10914 5

Printed in the UK by CPI Bookmarque, Croydon, Surrey
Papers used by Scholastic Children's Books are made from wood grown in
sustainable forests.

1 3 5 7 9 10 8 6 4 2

www.scholastic.co.uk/zone

Contents

Chapter 1
The Secret Under the Bed

Natty rode Ned at a steady canter beside the high wall of skirting board beneath her bed, before turning the pony across brown tuffets of carpet towards a jump of parallel poles. Except the poles weren't really poles but felt-tip pens, and the jump stands were made of old wooden cotton reels given to Natty by Mrs Plumley, who lived next door. The jump stood huge in front of them.

"Steady, Ned," Natty said.

"Don't worry," cried the chestnut pony, his mane and tail flying. "We'll clear this easily." He took off and Natty leaned into the jump with a big grin on her face. Doing showjumping under the bed was much better than being curled up under her duvet, which was where she had spent the first three days of the Christmas holidays ill with flu. Once they had landed, Ned slowed to a walk.

"That's enough for now. We've been round twice. Don't want to overdo it."

"We're not," said Natty. "I'm quite well again. It's just Mum who doesn't think so."

"You still sound a bit bunged up to me," said Ned, coming to a halt.

Natty pinched the end of her nose to stop a sneeze. She didn't manage it.

"Atishoo!"

"See what I mean?" said the chestnut pony.

If she was honest, her nose was still a bit tickly, but Natty knew

she was over the worst and Mum
had promised she could get up this
afternoon. It was brilliant that Ned
had chosen this morning to come
out of his poster. Any earlier in the
week and she would have felt too
ill to ride. Trust Ned to know the
best day to let his magic work. She
knew that while she lay flushed
and feverish, he had been keeping a
watchful eye on her from his pony
poster above her chest of drawers.

She flung her arms around his
neck, thinking how lucky she was to
have a magic pony of her very own.
One that went from big to small in

the blink of an eye, and could magic her tiny, too. How else would she be able to do showjumping under the bed? She had made the showjumps from her pencil case: two rulers, twelve cotton reels, her felt-tip pens and two bananas, which she was supposed to have eaten. Four jumps in all.

Lying flat on her tummy, she had set them up under the bed to keep them out of sight in case someone came in. She didn't think anyone would. Mum was busy downstairs on her knitting machine, and Jamie had gone to Ben's house to try out a new trick on his friend. Even so, it was best to be cautious. Her brother might come home unexpectedly, or Mum might come upstairs, silent as a mouse, and surprise her. Nobody but Natty knew that the chestnut pony in the poster could turn himself into a real live pony and, to keep Ned safe, nobody must ever find out. It was her most important and precious secret.

"Please, Ned, can't we go round just one more time?" Natty urged.

She was loath to get off, loving riding as she did, and much as she liked her cosy blue pyjamas, she preferred her magic riding clothes a million times more. Smart velvet crash hat, jodhpurs, jacket and jodhpur boots, which would all disappear the moment she dismounted and let go of the reins. "Please, Ned."

The pony let out a low whinny. "One last time and then it's back to bed," he said, and set off at a trot for the pencil-case jump, which was surprisingly big when you were a tiny rider on a tiny pony. Natty gave the jump her full attention and, with a squeeze of her heels, cantered Ned towards it.

"Here we go," he said. "One, two, three!" And he took off, soaring into the air, with a leap reaching almost as high as the mattress above them. Once again, Natty found herself grinning with pleasure. She turned her willing pony towards the banana spread, and was steering Ned straight for the centre of the jump when the door to her bedroom burst open.

"Hello, Natty, it's me!" Two giant feet wrapped in red woolly socks stood at the side of the bed.

"Help!" Natty gasped. Ned skidded to a stop on his haunches and Natty flung herself from his back on to a hillock of carpet and whispered, "It's Penelope Potter!"

"Natty, where are you?"

Knowing she had to return to her proper size as quickly as possible, and hoping Ned could get out of the way fast enough so as not to be squashed, Natty let go of the reins. With closed eyes she tumbled into a blast of magic wind, opening them again to find Penelope on hands and knees, staring straight at her.

"What are you doing all squashed up under there?" she asked. "I've come to see how you are."

Natty wriggled out from under the bed, leaving behind a demolished showjumping course but not, as far as she could tell, a flattened Ned. Back in her pyjamas, with her fluey red nose, she hardly looked the sort of person who, a few seconds ago, had been doing showjumping.

"I was just fetching my pencil case," she said, holding it up and hopping back into bed. She slid her feet under Tabitha, who uncurled and gave Penelope a thoughtful pussy-cat stare. "I'm going to do some drawing."

"Bit of a daft place to keep a pencil case, isn't it? Under the bed."

"It rolled there," said Natty, which was sort of true. "I'm surprised Mum let you come up in case you caught my bug."

"Oh, I told her I'd already had it so she let me."

"But you haven't!" said Natty, amazed at how easily Penelope told lies.

Penelope shrugged. "She's all in a tizzy anyway. Her knitting machine's broken or something." She flung her jacket on to the bed. "Besides, I won't get it now. Jamie said you were nearly better."

"I am," Natty agreed.

"Except for your red nose," Penelope smirked. "Does it glow in the dark?"

"All right! You don't have to go on about it," said Natty, thinking of Mum. It was the third time today her knitting machine had broken down and Natty knew she was worried she wouldn't finish all the jumpers she had to make in time for Christmas.

Something different about the window-sill caught Natty's eye. Instead of her usual three china ponies, lined up in a row looking out over the field opposite, there were four.

"Actually, I came to ask you a favour," said Penelope. "Can you help me get Pebbles's stable ready? I've been out with Mummy all morning and it's not even mucked out yet. I want to ride him before it snows."

"Is it going to?"

Natty instantly regretted the question. Penelope crossed to the window and leaned across the three china ponies and the tiny chestnut Ned to look out.

"The sky's full of horrid grey clouds and it's cold enough. So are you coming?"

"I would," said Natty, longing to get Penelope away from the window. "But I'm not allowed up yet. I will tomorrow if I can. Shall I make you a cup of hot chocolate?"

"Come and look at Pebbles. He's got his new winter rug on."

Natty jumped from the bed. She

would have to look or Penelope would never move. As it was, she was so close, she was almost touching Ned's back. Even worse, if she looked above the chest of drawers, she would see his empty poster.

"It's blue with a furry bit round the withers," Penelope said. "He could have had a green one but I thought blue would go better with his dapples. What do you think?"

"It's very nice," agreed Natty, glancing at the pretty grey pony strolling round the field. "I can make the chocolate in two ticks." She tugged at Penelope's arm.

"Come downstairs." But Penelope, being Penelope, wouldn't budge.

"Oh, I remember these. The china ponies with the funny names," she said, puckering her lips and tapping the window-sill with a finger. "What are they again? Prince, Percy and Tabitha!"

"No, Prince, Percy and Esmerelda! Tabitha's my cat." At the sound of her name Tabitha stood up, stretched and came to the edge of the bed. Taking aim, she leapt on to the chest of drawers.

"But you've got a new one. What's this chestnut one called? It's very lifelike." As Penelope leant forward to pick up Ned, Tabitha landed on her shoulders. That stopped her!

"Ouch! She's digging her claws in."

Purring loudly, Tabitha's front paws pounded while Penelope tried to shake the cat to the floor, which only made things worse.

"Get her off," she wailed. "I'm not a pincushion."

"Come on, Tabs," said Natty, clasping the cat's round middle. "It's her pussy-cat way of being friendly."

By the time Natty had prised Tabitha from Penelope's shoulder, the visitor was in a very bad mood.

"You ought to train that cat. It's got no manners. I'll probably need a blood transfusion after this."

"It just feels prickly when she kneads," said Natty. "It doesn't make you bleed."

"So you say." Penelope flounced towards the door. "After that, I think you should definitely help me muck out the stable – to make up!" She snatched her jacket from the bed.

"I will if I can," Natty called to the retreating figure stomping down the stairs. "Tomorrow!"

"Make sure you do."

Two seconds later, the front door slammed and, with a sigh of relief, Natty watched Penelope pull on her jacket and go crossly down the front path to the gate. Having Penelope live down the lane was sometimes a bit too close for comfort. She gave Tabitha a big cuddle, wondering if the fluffy cat knew she had saved Ned from discovery.

"Thanks, Puss," she said. "That was one narrow squeak!"

"It was rather, wasn't it?" said Ned, springing to life and trotting along the window-sill. Tabitha put out a paw to bat him in a rather half-hearted way. Dodging, he jumped towards the chest of drawers. A slight breeze ruffled the curtain and Ned was back in his poster – a picture pony again. By the time Mum popped her head round the door, everything was back to normal.

"Penelope didn't stay long," she said.

"No, she wanted me to help her with Pebbles. I said I could tomorrow."

"We'll see," was all Mum would say to that. "But if you feel well enough, you can get dressed now if you like."

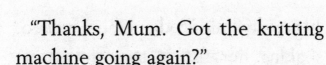

"Thanks, Mum. Got the knitting machine going again?"

"Just about."

"You really need a new one," said Natty.

"Wouldn't that be bliss? But this one's got to last. And don't stand by that window catching cold."

Natty was about to come away when there was an angry shout of "Road hogs!" from outside.

Four boys, taking up the whole of the lane with their bikes, had forced Penelope into the prickly hawthorn hedge before pedalling speedily in the direction of Winchway Wood.

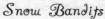

"Smelly pigs!" Penelope yelled, shaking her fist at their retreating backs. Natty could tell they'd done it on purpose by the boys' triumphant whoops.

It was Smudger Evans, Nick and Stew Taylor – the skinny twins – and Henry Henforth. For once, Natty agreed with Penelope. They were smelly pigs. The arrival of Smudger Evans and his gang always meant trouble. She was glad she was safe indoors.

Chapter 2
The Rope Trick

The next morning, Natty was woken up by a knock at her door. The light was switched on and Jamie bounded into the bedroom wearing his magician's cloak and waving his magician's top hat.

"Can I show you something?"

The first thing Natty realized, on

opening her eyes, was that Ned was still a glossy picture pony in his poster on her wall, so that was all right.

"Stay there and don't move. I've been up for ages practising. Prepare to be astonished."

Natty rubbed the sleep from her eyes and sat up. The second thing she realized was that it was only a quarter to eight. But it was nice to feel better. Her nose was clear and no longer sore where she'd been blowing it so much.

"OK," she said. "What is it?"

"It's called the magician's rope trick. I've perfected it. Watch this!"

From inside his top hat Jamie pulled out a piece of rope.

"*For my next trick...*"

"For your *only* trick," corrected Natty, whose thoughts were already racing ahead to the pleasing thought of helping Penelope. Looking after Pebbles was the perfect thing to do after days of being stuck indoors.

"All right, all right. *For my only trick, I would like a volunteer from the audience to assist me.*" There was a pause. "That's you, Natty."

"What do I do?"

"Hang on and I'll tell you. *Please, inspect this ordinary piece of rope.*"

Natty took the offered rope and wound it round her hand.

"Did you get it from Cosby's Magic Emporium?" she asked, knowing full well that Jamie had, and that it stood no chance at all of being an ordinary piece of rope but something that *looked* ordinary even though it was quite different. After all, hadn't her magic pony poster come from the very same place? And that was quite the most extraordinary thing she had come across in her whole life.

"Will you please stop interrupting," said Jamie, "and do as you're told."

Natty handed back the ordinary piece of rope.

"If you boss your audience about like that, they won't want to watch your show," she said.

Ignoring her, Jamie continued. "*As you can see, it's nothing but a bit of old rope. Or is it?*" He dropped the rope into his top hat, pulled his magician's wand from a pocket in his cloak, tapped the hat and recited these words:

"*Ropus diddle pocus,*
Dee diddle hocus dee."

Eyes alight with mystery, he placed the top hat on his head and, keeping as still as a statue, waited. By now, Natty was intrigued and wondered what was coming next. Even Tabitha, who had uncurled when Jamie came in, stopped washing her paw and stared at the hat.

It quivered and slowly lifted from the top of Jamie's head until there was a gap between the hat and his hair.

"Brilliant, Jamie!" cried Natty in admiration.

"Shush!" Jamie said between clenched teeth. He was concentrating hard.

Up went the hat, centimetre by centimetre, until Natty could see the rope straightening beneath it, lifting it higher. Then the hat began a slow spin and, as it spun, it slipped to a jaunty angle and appeared to settle as if hanging on an invisible hook, while the rope toppled to the floor.

"Oh, double elephants' bottoms," said Jamie, reaching up to snatch the hat. "Back to the drawing board." Natty suddenly saw the wire sticking up from the back of his neck.

"So it *is* just an ordinary piece of rope after all," she said.

"All magic is illusion and sleight of hand," said Jamie, picking up the offending rope. "But it's not quite an ordinary piece of rope. I'm doing something wrong. I wish I could work out what it is." And he marched from Natty's bedroom, then darted back in again. "You're sworn to secrecy, Natty. Tell no one about the wire." And he was gone again to have another practice.

"Mmm," said Natty, staring at Ned's poster. "I don't think Jamie's got it quite right about all magic being sleight of hand and illusion, do you, Ned? It seems to me there's magic tricks and real magic, and they're quite different from one another."

To her disappointment, the handsome chestnut pony didn't reply. Natty jumped from her bed with the sneaking feeling that Ned was going to remain in his picture all day. Never mind. Yesterday's showjumping had been a thrill and this morning she was going to help look after Pebbles, which was nearly as much fun as riding Ned.

After breakfast, when she had been wrapped up warmly by Mum and handed a bag of chopped carrots for Pebbles, Natty pulled on her wellington boots and hurried from the back door round the house to the lane. As she set off towards Penelope's stable yard, she looked up at her bedroom window and waved to her three china ponies, which she had put with their noses against the glass so they could see her go.

The sky was heavy with brooding

clouds and a chilly wind blew. In the front garden the bare branches of the fig tree rattled against the house wall. Penelope had been wrong about the snow yesterday, but would it fall today? Natty rubbed her gloved hands together and trotted on down the lane. It might.

In the stable yard she found Pebbles looking expectantly out over his stable door, blowing steamy breath down his nostrils. He whickered hopefully, expecting Natty to bring him his breakfast at last.

"Hello, Pebbles," she said, undoing the gate. She crossed to his stable, put her hand in the carrot bag and held out some finger-length pieces on a flat palm. Pebbles's gentle lips scooped them up and he was soon crunching contentedly. Natty stroked his dappled grey neck and breathed in the smell of horse. "I wonder where Penelope is?"

"I'm here," said Penelope, choosing this moment to cross the lane from the back drive of her house and arrive in the yard. "Haven't you started the mucking out yet?"

"I've only just got here," said Natty. It was obvious Penelope was in a bad mood. Her eyebrows were

drawn together in a deep frown.
"What's up?"

"What's up is that I was supposed
to be going ice skating with Trudi
this afternoon and now she can't
come. She's got your flu."

"It's not *my* flu," said Natty. "Lots of people have got it."

"I bet it is your flu. You breathed all over both of us on the school bus last week. I shouldn't wonder if I don't get it next."

"That's not fair," said Natty. "If you're going to be like that, I'm going home."

"You said you'd help with the mucking out."

"Do it yourself."

Natty was almost at the gate when Penelope darted across the yard and took hold of her arm.

"Don't go, Natty. I was only

joking. I didn't really mean it was your fault. Honestly." Natty waited to see what was coming next. It was a smile, one of Penelope's real charmers. "Actually, I'm going to take Pebbles out on a hack in Winchway Wood later. Why don't you come along, too? I'll let you have a little ride, if you do."

Pebbles gave another low whicker, nodding his head over the stable door as if asking her to stay too. Natty relented. The thought of even a *little* ride on Pebbles was tempting, and Penelope didn't often make such an offer.

"OK," said Natty. "I'll fetch the wheelbarrow. I think Pebbles wants his breakfast."

"I'm getting it now," said Penelope, satisfied that her persuading tactics had worked. "And after you've done the mucking out, you can help groom him if you like."

It was after Pebbles had eaten his bucket of pony nuts and was tucking into a fresh hay-net that Jamie sped into the yard on his bike.

"Just to remind you, Natty. Not a word to anyone about the rope trick."

"I promise," said Natty, giving a

meaningful glance in the direction
of the stable, where Penelope was
collecting Pebbles's empty bucket.
Jamie took the hint but too late.
Penelope was outside in a second.

"What rope trick? Can I see it?"

"You can if you come to the village
Christmas Show," said Jamie, turning
his bike.

"I could be your assistant if you
like," she offered. "I'm frightfully
good at keeping secrets." Which
was not what either Natty or Jamie
thought at all.

"I don't need an assistant, thanks,"
said Jamie and he was gone before

Penelope could utter another word.

"But conjurers always have pretty assistants," pouted Penelope. "And I've got a lovely dress. See if you can persuade him for me, Natty, will you?"

Natty shrugged. "He won't change his mind if it's made up."

"He will if you ask him."

Natty laughed. "Not a chance!"

"Promise me you'll try."

Natty looked at Penelope's eager face and relented.

"OK," she said. "I'll try." And, taking hold of the wheelbarrow, she trundled it to the dungheap.

Chapter 3
The Buckled Wheel

When Natty had finished pitch-forking the steaming heap into a tidy shape, she stood on top of it and wriggled her wellingtons into the dung. The further down she wriggled, the warmer it got, and her toes were toasting nicely when she heard the bumping of another wheelbarrow coming into the yard.

"Lambkin, I need a couple of barrowloads of rotted manure to put round my new saplings. I don't want the frost killing them. See to that, can you?" It was Mr Potter.

"Natty'll do them. She's round at the dungheap now. We'll bring them up when she's finished."

"Thank you, Penny Wenny Pops!"

Natty couldn't help grinning. She had never heard Mr Potter call Penelope Penny Wenny Pops before. Luckily her dad never called her anything that daft. But the grin faded as she realized what a lot of digging it would take to fill two wheelbarrows with dung. Still, it would warm her up. Pulling out her toasting toes, she made her way to the well-rotted end of the heap and got to work with the pitchfork.

"Thanks, Natty," said Mr Potter, trundling his garden barrow round the stable to find her. "You heard my request?" Natty nodded shyly as he put his wheelbarrow next to the stable barrow. "Two loads will be plenty."

Having to do so much digging meant that Natty completely missed the chance to help with grooming Pebbles. By the time she had finished, he was fully brushed with his hooves picked out. Glowing with a rosy warmth right to the ends of her fingertips, she stood next to the two full wheelbarrows – ready to help push one up the gravel of the Potters' back drive.

"He's all done," said Penelope, closing the stable door. Pebbles leaned out to view the world, wisps of hay hanging from his lips, before turning back for another pull at his hay-net.

"I know," said Natty wistfully. "I saw you take the grooming box back to the tack room."

"Oh, silly me, I'd forgotten you like to do grooming. If I'd remembered, I'd have done the digging."

Natty knew Penelope too well to believe that. She was used to hearing her say she'd do something after someone else had already done it and, picking up the handles of the nearest wheelbarrow, she set off for Mr Potter's garden.

The lane was empty when she crossed it, apart from Tabitha, who scampered from Pebbles's field into her own garden, probably on her way indoors to sit by the fire. Natty crunched a little way along the gravel drive before realizing Penelope was not following. She put down the barrow and waited.

A robin hopped along the gate towards her. It was very tame and no doubt wondering if it would find a juicy worm in the newly dug manure. To welcome the robin, Natty took a couple of steps backwards and, to pass the time, blew steam balloons. The little bird swooped and, after some serious pecking in the dung, flew off again with a pink worm wriggling in its beak. Fed up with waiting, Natty went back to find out what was holding Penelope up.

She heard the bikes before she saw them. Rubber on tarmac, swooshing to the rhythm of feet on pedals, then the shriek of rubber on metal as the brakes went on, and there they were, ringing the yard gate, blocking Penelope's way out – Smudger Evans and his gang! Natty's heart skipped a beat. What did they want?

Holding the handles of her wheelbarrow, Penelope gave the leering boys an icy stare.

"Get out of my way," she ordered.

"Get out of my way," mimicked Smudger in a silly voice.

"I'm warning you," said Penelope, a frown deepening on her forehead, her eyes narrowing. Danger signs, Natty knew.

"Do you hear that, Nick?" guffawed Smudger. "She's warning me."

"Do you hear that, Stew?" said Nick, passing on the message in a monotone to his twin.

"I hear it," said Stew, receiving the message in the same deadpan way.

"I hear it too," said Henry, not wanting to be left out. "She's warning you, Smudge!"

With a sudden jerk of his bike, Smudger rammed the wheelbarrow, sending a clod of dung to the ground.

"Who's a smelly pig now?" he asked.

"Don't be mean, Smudger, let her go."

At the sound of Natty's voice, Smudger swung round.

"Oh, look, little Natty Deakin to the rescue! Can't your smelly-pig friend look after herself, is that it?"

All four boys turned to look at Natty. None of them saw Penelope take a few paces backwards or the determined gleam in her eye. It was only by the look on Natty's face that they realized something was up, and by that time Penelope was charging.

"GET OUT OF MY WAY!" she yelled at the top of her voice. The boys backed off fast, but Smudger was too late. The barrow clipped his front wheel and he and the bike toppled to the ground. The wheelbarrow reared up – whether helped by Penelope or not, Natty didn't know – and the whole load of manure slid out on top of him.

"Now look what you've made me do, you great lump of blubber," Penelope yelled. "Muck all over the place."

Smudger jumped up, spitting and shaking, not having bargained for Penelope's spirited action. His gang rallied round, quickly dropping their bikes to brush off the offending muck with their fingertips and mutter dire threats under their breath.

"I'll get you for this, Penelope Potter," Smudger growled darkly. "You see if I don't."

"Oh, grow up," snapped Penelope, and marched back into the stable yard.

"What did you say?" said Smudger, shaking off his cleaners and following her.

"You heard, fat porker. I said grow up."

By now, Natty was thoroughly alarmed. Penelope was pushing her luck beyond all bounds. Why couldn't she see that, under his coating of manure, Smudger was white with rage?

But the moment Penelope took hold of the pitchfork, Smudger stopped in his tracks.

"What do you think you're going to do with that?" he asked, suddenly not so sure of himself.

"Find out if the fat porker goes pop!" said Penelope menacingly.

Smudger backed off. "Stupid boy! Pick up the manure – what else? I should make you do it. It was your fault the wheelbarrow tipped up."

Smudger snatched at his handlebars and lifted up his bike. He let out a howl of rage.

"You snail brain!" He lashed out with his boot, sending the wheelbarrow flying. "You've buckled the front wheel." He limped a couple of steps. "It'll cost loads for a new one. You'll to have to pay."

"No chance," said Penelope, handing the stunned Natty the pitchfork and picking up the wheelbarrow. "Just get out of the way so we can get this muck back in the barrow."

Natty forked with haste. She wanted to get to the safety of the garden as fast as she could. It was a relief when Mr Potter crunched down the drive.

"What's all the shouting about?" he asked. "You all right, Penelope?"

"No thanks to this lot," she said. "They made me spill manure all over the lane."

Mr Potter turned to the glowering Smudger, who picked up his bike and signalled retreat. It was all very well for Penelope to look smug.

Natty knew this was the start of something. Smudger would never forget such a devastating defeat. Why didn't Penelope know that?

"Well, you seem to have seen them off," said Mr Potter with a smile.

"Haven't I just," said Penelope.

For now, thought Natty. *But they'll be back.* She didn't say anything to Penelope or Mr Potter, but she was scared. Smudger would want revenge.

Chapter 4
The Warning

Natty pushed the empty wheel-barrow back into the stable yard and dumped it by the hay-shed door. She stood the pitchfork beside it. She had spread the manure around the roots of Mr Potter's saplings and felt she had done enough.

"Where are you off to?" Penelope asked, arriving back from the garden.

"There's something I've got to do."

"Can't it wait? I thought you were coming riding with me." Penelope headed for the tack room to fetch Pebbles's saddle and bridle.

"Another time." Natty glanced wistfully at the dapple grey pony leaning out over the stable door.

"What do you mean, another time? Is that all the thanks I get?"

"Penelope," said Natty, "you don't seem to realize what you've done! Smudger is not going to leave things. Not after what happened today."

"Oh, don't go on about Smudger. He started it. It wasn't my fault his beastly bike got broken." There was no denying that Smudger had caused the trouble but Penelope had finished it in a dramatic and, for Smudger, humiliating way. "Serves him right. He's always having a go. Maybe now he'll leave me alone."

"But what happens if it has the opposite effect?" Natty asked. "What if he doesn't leave you alone?"

"If he tries anything, Daddy will sort him out."

That was all very well, but Mr Potter would have to catch him first. Smudger was a slippery eel, and being covered with horse dung and going home with a buckled front wheel was enough to set anyone fuming, let alone him. Natty wasn't taking any chances.

"I'm going to warn Jamie."

"Whatever for?"

"Because Smudger's his worst enemy," said Natty, setting off at a run.

"Just don't forget to ask if I can be his assistant!"

With Penelope's request ringing

in her ears, Natty raced down the
lane to the main road, her eyes
peeled for Smudger and the other
gang members in case they decided
to come back. She guessed that
Jamie had gone to Ben's house, and,
running into the village, she hurried
past the phone box and the shop.

Opposite the church she turned into Farley Crescent. Ben's house was the last house at the bottom with the red front door. Natty sped up the path and knocked. There was no reply; only barking from Bouser, the fat beagle that belonged to Ben's mum.

Natty looked through the letter box.

"Hello, Bouser, anyone at home?"

Bouser stopped barking, gave a couple of snuffles, and wandered off towards the kitchen. Natty let the letter box drop. She had almost given up when she heard footsteps in the hall and the door opened a fraction. A face peeped through the chink.

"Oh, it's you, Natty," said Ben, opening the door wider.

"Is Jamie there?"

Ben nodded and stood back for her to come in. "Is something up?"

It was Natty's turn to nod. She pulled off her wellington boots and left them on the mat. It was warm in the house and she unwound her scarf and unbuttoned her jacket.

"Who is it?" It was Ben's new dad calling from the back room.

"It's Natty for Jamie," Ben replied. He pointed upstairs. "Come up."

Bouser had waddled back down the hallway to give Natty a sniff, and she gave his head and his silky ears a stroke. Satisfied, he lay down on the hall carpet with a grunt. Natty padded up the stairs in her socks and followed Ben into the back bedroom. Jamie looked up from the floor, where he was doing something fiddly with a piece of rope.

"Hi, Natty. Giving Penelope Potter a miss?"

"Only because of Smudger Evans," said Natty. "Which is a bit of a nuisance because Penelope was going to let me ride Pebbles this morning."

"What's happened?" Jamie asked. Having mentioned Smudger Evans, both boys were giving her their full attention. Natty sat on the end of Ben's bed and suddenly fell back in a burst of delicious laughter.

"Tell us then," said Ben.

"Yes, come on, Natty, share the joke," said Jamie.

It took Natty ages before she could speak. All she could think of was Smudger underneath the pile of dung and it was terribly, terribly funny.

"It was Penelope," she spluttered, eyes sparkling. "She covered Smudger with a whole barrowload of dung."

"What?" said Ben, his face lighting up.

"How?" Jamie asked.

"We were taking manure to the garden for Mr Potter's saplings. Smudger and the gang blocked off the yard gate and wouldn't let Penelope out. She came at them like a bat out of hell, rammed Smudger's bike and – wham! – Smudger was covered."

The boys let out huge whoops and punched each other before leaping backwards and forwards across the bed shouting, "Penelope Potter for President! Penelope Potter for President!"

It wasn't until they'd calmed down a bit that Natty went on, her own glee fading as she spoke.

"The bad news is that she buckled his front wheel. He's going to have to get a new one."

"That'll teach him," chuckled Ben.

Jamie couldn't stop grinning either. "Never meddle with Penelope Potter!" he said.

"But Jamie, Smudger's out for revenge. He's really mad. He looked evil when he went."

They took in Natty's serious expression.

"You're right, Natty. He won't let this go," Jamie said. "We're on red alert. OK?"

"How about a spot of spying?" suggested Ben. "See if we can find out what they're going to do."

"First thing, he'll get his bike fixed for sure," said Jamie.

"Or not," said Ben. "He'll nab Henry's if he's desperate."

"He'll still want to get his own

fixed. And a new wheel costs pounds."

"Too right," said Ben.

"But Smudger doesn't have pounds," said Jamie. "Which means he won't be able to get it fixed."

Ben ran his fingers through his hair. "He might try and steal one of ours."

"Yes, a spot of spying's the thing," agreed Jamie. "We've got to find out."

"Can I come?" Natty asked as the boys got up to go.

"You haven't got a bike," said Ben.

"Jamie can give me a backie."

Jamie looked doubtful.

"If you don't it won't be fair. I told you what happened."

"Oh, all right," Jamie said. "If you must."

"And Penelope said please can she be your assistant? She's got a really nice dress," said Natty, remembering her promise.

"Penelope Potter for President – yes! Penelope Potter for my assistant – no!" It was exactly the answer Natty had expected.

76

Chapter 5
Spying

It wasn't until Natty's legs were swinging from either side of Jamie's bike saddle that she wondered if she'd made the right move. Spying on the boys, Jamie had told her, meant riding round to the allotments, hiding the bikes and creeping up to Smudger's dad's shed, where Smudger and the gang met. Now they were actually heading there, she felt a surge of panic, as if they were going to put their heads into a lion's mouth or do something equally scary.

She calmed herself with the thought that the gang probably wouldn't be there; that they would be somewhere else trying to get Smudger's bike fixed. She took a deep breath and held it as Jamie leaned into a bend so sharp that her boot grazed the tarmac. He straightened the bike and braked hard. They had arrived.

The allotments lay behind the row of houses where Smudger lived. Now it was winter there was not much ground cover. The only vegetables growing were gangly Brussels sprouts, a few cabbages and leeks. The earth was iron-hard. The sky was ominously dark and the muffled stillness made Natty feel they would be easily overheard.

Jamie and Ben, silent as the tracker scouts they no doubt imagined they were, dropped their bikes into the ditch, then signalled for her to follow through a gap in the hedge. Clearly they had been here before.

Pushing through the hawthorn prickles, Natty shielded her face, pulling against the thorns that snagged her jacket.

Bent double, she ran after the two boys. For a moment, all three crouched behind a row of bean sticks bearing nothing but the remnants of dried-out stalks. It was sparse cover.

"A briefing," whispered Jamie. "See the old black shed? That one. Directly behind Smudger's garden. They're in there."

Natty's heart skipped a beat for the second time that day.

"H-h-how do you know?" she stuttered, trying to pull herself together.

"'Cos of the bikes."

Of course, now they were pointed out, she could see them, three bikes leaning against a pair of rusty barrels.

"How about letting a few tyres down?" suggested Ben.

"Good idea," said Jamie.

"I thought we were going to listen?" Natty said.

"Safety precaution. If their tyres are flat, they can't cycle after us."

Natty swallowed nervously. What had she let herself in for? Well, she was here now, and she wanted to find out what the gang intended to do about Penelope. "You let the tyres down. I'll listen."

"You're on," said Jamie, and he sprinted forward for the next bit of cover, which was a large compost heap. They arrived one after the other. Panting slightly, Jamie said, "There's no more cover until the shed. Ready to do the tyres, Ben?" Ben nodded and they were off.

Natty's legs were the shortest and she arrived at the shed last. All three of them crouched low, catching their breath, waiting to see if they'd been heard. From inside came the steady drone of voices, then one raised in an angry shout.

Slowly, Natty moved closer to the corrugated iron wall, her breath coming in steamy puffs, her blood pulsing in her ears.

A single snowflake drifted down
and landed on her sleeve. From the
three bikes came an angry hissing
as the tyres were let down. The
missing bike was Smudger's; the
broken one.

"I said pull it, Henry," shouted the
irate voice from inside the shed.

"*I – am – pulling,*" came the reply.

"Henry, you're pathetic. Stew,
get hold of it and help him." There
was a silence filled with grunts and
heaves and then a crash.

"Ouch!"

"Done it!"

"The tyre's off, Smudge. What

next?" That was Nick or Stew. Natty couldn't tell which.

"We'll bash it straight."

"You never will. It needs a new wheel."

"Shut it, Henry. I know it needs a new wheel but I've got to get the money first, and that might take a few days."

"I was only saying."

"Well, don't. Say nothing at all. I'm not in the mood."

"The Potters should pay by rights." That was a twin.

"Oh, they will," said Smudger. "They will."

"Lots of money?"

"Yes, Henry, my lad. Lots of money. I got a plan all worked out."

"That's brilliant, Smudge. For pounds and pounds?"

"Yes, Henry, for pounds and pounds."

"The Potters are rolling, Smudge. You could have a new bike!"

"There is one little thing to be done first, Henry."

"What's that?"

"Before we get any money, we have to take a – what shall I call it? – a hostage."

"A hostage? Yeah! They pay the money to get the hostage back.

Brilliant, Smudge. I bet I know who that's going to be!"

Natty's ears were burning. She had the awful feeling she knew too.

"I bet you don't, Henry."

"I do, I do. It's going to be…"

There was a metallic bang as Ben tripped over a pedal and one of the bikes toppled against a barrel. The noise sent Jamie and Ben running. Natty, left behind, darted round the shed and crouched out of sight as the door was pulled open. If only Ned were here! She could jump on his back, be magicked small, and hide under the shed.

Jamie glanced over his shoulder but had enough sense not to give her away. Natty knew she could never outrun Nick and Stew, and it was touch and go if Jamie and Ben would. Smudger and Henry were jumping up and down, urging them on. Then Nick tripped and went sprawling and Stew stopped to see if his twin was all right. Jamie and Ben scrambled through the hedge and, a few seconds later, Natty saw them glide along the lane on their bikes.

Now what was she going to do? She slunk against the shed, hardly daring to breathe.

"We should have brought the bikes in, Smudge," said Henry. "They've done the usual."

"So they have. Get pumping, then."

Henry sighed. "Right you are, Smudge."

"You two all right?" Smudger asked as the twins came back.

"Yeah! You saw who it was?" said Nick.

"We'll deal with them another time. We've got more important things to see to."

"Do you think they heard anything?" Stew asked.

"Nah, not all the tyres are flat. They

didn't finish, see, before they got clumsy. Henry can stay outside and keep watch while he's pumping."

"Come off it, Smudge. It's snowing."

And it was. More and more fluffy flakes were dropping from the silent sky.

"All right," said Smudger, relenting. "Bring the bikes in. Deakin and his crony won't dare come back after that botch-up."

Natty stayed behind the shed until she was sure that all four boys were inside and the door was shut. She didn't wait to hear any more. She had heard enough. They were planning to kidnap Penelope and hold her to ransom. Penelope had to be warned. The snow was falling faster now. Pulling her scarf over her head, and keeping low, she quickly made her way back to the gap in the hedge.

Chapter 6
Kidnap

Jamie and Ben were waiting for her on the corner opposite the church, hunched up against the falling snow.

"What took you so long?" asked Jamie with a grin.

"I could have been captured, for all you care," said Natty, shaking snow from her scarf.

"You were quite safe," said Ben. "We doubled back and checked." Natty wasn't sure she believed them.

"We did," said Jamie. "We saw you and watched the gang take the bikes into the shed. By now Henry will be busy pumping."

"How do you know it'll be Henry?"

"Because when we let the tyres down it's always Henry who pumps them up again."

"That's not fair!"

"Nat, when is Smudger ever fair? Now come on, what did you hear?"

Jamie flicked snow from his fringe and looked at her eagerly.

A trickle of melted snow ran down Natty's nose. She brushed it off and took a deep breath.

"They're going to take Penelope hostage. They want the Potters to give them lots of money so Smudger can buy a new bike!" The boys stared at her as if she were crazy.

"They'll never get away with it," said Jamie, shaking his head.

"But that's what they're planning."

"Jumping jackasses!" said Ben, suddenly coming to life. "They're daft enough to try."

"Quite," said Natty. "And before we all turn into snowmen, I think we ought to warn Penelope."

"Where is she?" Jamie asked.

"Out riding Pebbles. But now it's snowing she's probably on her way back."

"Jump on, Nat. We'll find her. At least we can put her on her guard."

"On the other hand," said Ben, "it might be a bit of a hoot, old P. Potter getting ransomed. It would get rid of her for a bit."

"Don't be so mean. Would you fancy being kidnapped in the snow? It's freezing."

"Natty's right. She could die of hypo-thingy."

"Of what?" Natty asked.

"Hypothermia," said Ben, who was good with words. "You get it when you're freezing cold."

"Hypothermia! Exactly!" said Natty. "That's why we've got to warn her."

Jamie moved forward on to his crossbar and waited for Natty to climb on to the saddle. Several snowflakes got there first and she brushed them off. Already the pavement was turning white.

"Be careful when you go round a corner, Jamie. It'll be slippery."

"Trust me," said Jamie and pedalled hard. This was all very well, because Natty knew that already he was going too fast. She clung on to the back of his jacket and gritted her teeth. The main road had been salted and was snow-free but the moment they turned into the lane the back wheel skidded. Jamie righted the bike and kept pedalling.

"Slow down," Natty yelled. She was too late, and when they turned into Penelope's stable yard, the saddle went from under her. Natty managed to land on her feet but Jamie collapsed with the bike, and came slithering to a stop in front of Penelope.

Alarmed by the clatter, Pebbles backed into his stable, but when all the noise had stopped he put his head out to see what was going on. With a bridle over her shoulder and a saddle over her arm, Penelope hauled on Jamie's jacket with her free hand in an attempt to help him up.

"Get off," he said ungraciously.

Penelope let go. "I was only trying to help," she said huffily, and carried on to the tack room, leaving Jamie to clamber up by himself.

"I did say to be careful," said Natty.

"All right, clever clogs." Jamie inspected his bike for damage.

Ben leaned on his handlebars, grinning, but was sensible enough not to say anything. The bike seemed unharmed and Jamie leant it against the snow-covered mudguard of the horse trailer.

"Penelope?"

"What?" said Penelope, coming out of the tack room with a hoof pick. "And don't put your bike there – it might scratch the trailer."

Jamie removed his bike, which only made Ben grin more.

"We've come to warn you," said Natty, jumping in before things got worse. "Smudger Evans and the gang are planning to kidnap you and hold you to ransom."

Penelope stopped dead in her tracks. "What?" she said, and let out a peal of mocking laughter. "I'd like to see them try."

"We're warning you, that's all,"

said Jamie. "So you can be on your guard." He wheeled his bike towards the gate, weaving a snake-like track in the snow.

"He wants ransom money to pay for a new bike," added Natty. "He's planning the kidnap now."

"Well," said Penelope, "he can whistle for his ransom money. He's not getting a penny from me, I can tell you."

Jamie and Ben exchanged a look and shrugged their shoulders as if to say, *There's nothing more we can do*.

"That's it," said Natty, her eyes lighting up. "A whistle!"

"Now what are you on about?" said Penelope, brushing snow from her jacket and going into the stable. "I'm going to pick out Pebbles's feet before I forget."

Natty turned back to the boys. "We could have a signal. A whistle signal."

"As a danger signal?" said Ben.

"Yes, three long blasts. Something like that," said Natty. "Then if any of us hears it, we know to watch out for Smudger, and that whoever is whistling needs help."

"I haven't got a whistle," said Penelope, leaning over the stable door.

"You don't need one if you can do this," said Jamie, and, putting a thumb and forefinger into his mouth, he blew a shrill blast. Ben did the same in reply.

"Can you do it, Natty?" he asked.

"Not yet." She had been trying

for ages but still could only manage a hiss. "But I have got a referee's whistle that Dad gave me. That would do."

"Well, I can't whistle through my fingers and I haven't got any other sort of whistle, so that's that," said Penelope.

"I'll lend you mine," said Natty. "After all, you're the one who's going to be kidnapped."

"I am not!"

Natty ignored her. "Two long blasts means danger! Three means help!"

Jamie blew two practice blasts through his fingers.

"Agreed," he said, and smiled at Penelope. "What do you think?" And the smile did the trick.

"Oh, all right," she said. "Natty can give me her whistle just in case. But I know I won't need it."

Natty pulled off a glove and tried blowing through her numb fingers. Nothing. Drying them against the inside leg of her jeans, she tried again. For the first time ever there was a shrill piping; not loud, not long, but a whistle sure enough.

"Hey, I did it," she said, grinning with pleasure. "I'll keep practising and then we'll all be able to do the signal. I'll get you the referee's whistle straight away."

"Don't bother bringing it down. I'll come with you now and fetch it."

Natty glanced at Penelope with surprise and found her smiling at Jamie. Jamie looked stonily at his handlebars. Natty hoped she wasn't going to ask to be his assistant again. She didn't stand a chance. As if anticipating the request, Jamie suddenly flung himself on to his bike.

"I've got to go back to your house, Ben. I've left the rope trick." And he pedalled out of the yard and off down the lane.

"See you," Ben said, weaving more snake-like tracks as he followed.

The two girls walked to Natty's house side by side. The snow was not coming down so fast now, but there was enough on the ground for it to crunch satisfyingly underfoot.

"I'd like to build a snowman in the back garden," said Natty, scooping up a powdery handful and making her cold fingers tingle as she patted it into a snowball. Penelope made no comment. It was her turn to look stony, and Natty guessed she was upset at Jamie's sudden departure. She threw the snowball into the hedge, where it knocked snow from the leafless branches. "And then go to Winchway Wood and toboggan down the Ups and Downs." Still no response from Penelope.

Natty hadn't been to the Ups and Downs for ages, but now there was snow it was the best place she could think of for making toboggan slides. She looked up at the sky, not wanting the snow to stop. The thought of speeding downhill on the old toboggan was thrilling. She would fetch the whistle for Penelope, then go to the garden shed and find it. After that she would shut herself in her bedroom and tell Ned everything that had happened.

Chapter 7
Danger Signal

It didn't work out quite as she planned. The moment Natty put her head around the living-room door Mum looked up from her knitting machine and pounced.

"Look at those wet jeans," she said. "And you've been in bed with flu for three days. Go on, straight upstairs and into a hot bath with you."

"But Mum, I'm fine. Penelope's here. I've got to fetch something for her and then I'm going to get out the old toboggan."

Mum looked out of the window. "Oh, my goodness," she said. "It's snowing!"

It was a surprise that Mum hadn't noticed before but then, once she was knitting, she didn't notice anything much. It wasn't until she stopped that she was her usual observant self.

"Where is Penelope?"

"At the back door. She doesn't want to come in."

"Be quick and fetch whatever it is. I'll go up and run a bath."

Natty knew there was no arguing and, if she was honest, she was feeling tired. It had been an adventurous morning and the toboggan would have to wait. She followed Mum upstairs and fetched the whistle from her bookshelf. Ned looked out from his poster with pricked ears as if waiting for news.

"I'll be back in two ticks," she whispered, and hurried downstairs to the back door.

"What was the signal again?" Penelope asked.

Natty handed her the whistle. "Two loud blasts for danger. Three for help."

Penelope put the end of the whistle between her teeth and blew. Natty covered her ears. The sound was piercing.

"Easy. Three blasts for help. That'll bring the boys running."

"And me," said Natty. "So don't blow unless you have to."

"Oh, yes, and you," said Penelope. "Well, I'm off to sort out my skating stuff. It's a pain having to go on my own but there it is." And she put the whistle in her pocket and trudged back along the path, adding to the snowy footprints they had already made around the house.

Natty hurried upstairs to talk to Ned, still a picture in his poster.

She would have preferred him to be a prancing pony on her carpet, but even though he wasn't, he was looking straight at her, with an alert and interested expression. Natty checked the landing. Mum was in the bathroom swishing the bathwater. She dodged back into her bedroom and closed the door.

"You'll never guess what!" she said. "Smudger Evans and his gang are planning to kidnap Penelope Potter and all because Smudger's front wheel got buckled." Footsteps came towards the door. "I'll tell you the rest later." Natty sat on the bed and pulled off her socks so that she was busy when Mum came in.

"Chop-chop, Natty. Wet clothes off. You look blue with cold."

"I'll soon warm up in the bath," said Natty, pulling off her sweater. She scampered along the landing to the bathroom, shedding the rest of her clothes as she went.

After a luxurious hot soak, Natty sat on her bed and gazed at Ned. Her cheeks were glowing and she was surprisingly sleepy. Fighting a yawn, she told Ned the rest of the story. It was important he knew that Smudger planned to ransom

Penelope for lots of money and that two long blasts of the whistle meant danger and three meant help.

"Not that I can do anything about it today. Mum says I've been out enough and I've got to stay indoors until tomorrow. Boring! Especially when I wanted to make a snowman and go tobogganing. I just hope the snow lasts." She gave another yawn. "There's hours to wait until tomorrow." She fell back on her pillow, grabbing her book. "Still, they won't be able to kidnap Penelope this afternoon. She's going ice-skating." And she began to read.

But by the time Tabitha squeezed round the door and snuggled up beside her, Natty was fast asleep.

When she finally woke up it was dark, the light was on and the curtains were drawn. Mum was sitting on the edge of the bed watching her.

"You've had a good long sleep," she said. "Dad and Jamie are home and it's teatime."

Natty struggled to sit up.

"Has anyone been whistling?" she asked, rubbing her eyes.

"Whistling?" said Mum. "No, not that I know of. If you've heard whistling, you must have dreamed it."

Natty didn't try and explain. Ned was still in his poster so he couldn't tell her. She pulled on her slippers and followed Mum downstairs. In the living room Jamie was twiddling with a piece of rope and, at the same time, puzzling over an instruction leaflet.

"Still having trouble?" Natty asked, watching Mum go into the kitchen to join Dad, who was helping.

"I'm getting there," said Jamie, looking up. "I wish I could afford to buy a Vanishing Box Trick. It would be my magic act's star attraction."

"What does it do?"

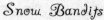

"It's a box with a door and you put something in it, like a cat – Tabby would do – or someone's best watch. Then you make it vanish."

"Then what do you do?"

"You make it come back again, of course. Mr Cosby's got one in his shop but it costs loads." He sighed. "Dream on, Jamie Deakin." Then he went back to his instruction leaflet before looking up again. "By the way, I've got out the old toboggan. It's ready by the back door. If the snow lasts, we can have some fun with it tomorrow."

"Any sign of Smudger and the

others?" Natty asked, raising the question that was most worrying her.

"I saw Penelope in the stable yard just now. Back from skating, she said. No problems. They wouldn't dare kidnap her. Smudger's not that stupid. Everyone would know it was him."

Natty would have liked to have believed Jamie, but when she was listening to Smudger outside the hut he had sounded so vehement. Perhaps he had changed his mind. She went into the kitchen to give Dad a hug, hoping she was right.

* * *

There was more snow in the night and the next morning the world was hidden beneath a thick white blanket. It looked so inviting that Natty hardly had the patience to wait until after breakfast, she was so eager to go outside. Once she was allowed to, she bounded up the stairs to her bedroom to get ready. Ned's poster was empty and she found him trotting across the window-sill towards her, tossing his head in greeting.

"Time for some snowballing, Natty," he said. "And a trot through the wintery woods."

"Yes, please," said Natty, thrilled to see him. "And Jamie's got out the old toboggan."

"Then what are we waiting for?" said the pony, jumping from the window-sill into the front pocket of Natty's rucksack, ready to be taken out of the house in secret.

Natty and Jamie were both by the back door pulling on their wellington boots when, shrill on the sharp morning air, they heard a whistle blast. They looked at one another. Then came a second and a third. There was a sudden scramble and a race round the house to the side gate.

From the direction of Penelope's stable yard came three more blasts. Jamie put his fingers to his mouth and blew a long whistle back.

With her rucksack bouncing on her back, Natty scrunched through the thick snow as fast as her legs would take her, arriving in the stable yard just before Jamie and bumping into a frantic Penelope.

"What's up?" she asked.

Tears streaked Penelope's cheeks and the words "He's gone" burst out between huge sobs.

"Who's gone?" asked Jamie.

"Pebbles!"

But Natty could already see that.
The stable door was wide open
and snow had drifted up against
it, wedging it to the wall. The door

looked as though it had been like that for ages.

"However did he get out?" exclaimed Natty.

"He didn't get out," cried Penelope. "He's been stolen."

"How do you know?" asked Jamie.

"Because his headcollar and lead rope have gone and the yard gate was left open as well."

"We can follow his tracks in the snow," said Natty. "He may not be far away and you don't know for sure he was stolen."

"Somebody let him out, and if they let him out, they stole him. I know it. And there are no tracks. The snow's covered everything."

Mr Potter came hurrying into the yard to find out what was the matter. At once Penelope flung herself upon him, sobbing and unable to speak.

"Whatever is it, my lambkin?" he asked.

"Pebbles is gone and Penelope thinks he's been stolen," said Natty, hurrying to explain.

Mr Potter glanced towards the empty stable and his face fell.

"We'll ring the police straight away," he said.

"And we'll go and look for him,"

said Jamie. "I'll get Ben to help. It's possible he's not gone far."

Natty had a sudden sinking feeling that she had got something wrong, but she couldn't think what it was. Anyway, the most important thing for now was to find Pebbles. And leaving Mr Potter to comfort Penelope as best he could, she followed Jamie from the yard and turned in the opposite direction.

"I'll look for tracks," she called, and plodded purposefully in the direction of Winchway Wood.

Chapter 8
Search

"Stop a minute, Natty," said Ned, poking his head from the rucksack pocket. "Most curious. I think we can safely say that if it was horse thieves, they didn't take Pebbles away in a lorry."

"How do you know?" Natty asked.

"If a lorry had come along the

lane from the main road, we would see where the wheels had been, even under the fresh snow. There's no hint of any ruts. But there are footprints. The new ones made this morning are obvious, but there are older ones the fresh snow's covered. You can tell by the way the snow dips."

"Yes," said Natty. "Lots of dips means lots of footprints, and there are loads."

"And going in both directions too," said Ned.

"So some must be Pebbles's hoofprints."

"Indeed, Natty, they must, leading straight into Winchway Wood if I've got this right."

Natty followed the footprints along the lane. She was just passing the house next to theirs when the front door opened and their neighbour called out.

"Yoo-hoo, Natty!"

Natty smiled and waved. "Hello, Mrs Plumley."

At the sound of Natty's voice a little white dog squeezed round Mrs Plumley's legs, jumped to the path and raced through the snow to the gate.

"Hello, Ruddles," said Natty as the little dog leapt up to lick her.

"Can you take the little scamp for a walk, Natty dear?" smiled Mrs Plumley, holding up a dog lead. "My old legs don't like the snow and Ruddles is longing to go out."

"We're searching for Pebbles," said Natty, opening the gate and going up the path to collect the lead. "He's gone missing. Probably stolen."

"Oh, goodness me, what a terrible thing!" said Mrs Plumley. Ruddles bounced up and down with excitement, and the moment Natty clipped on the lead he pulled to go.

"That poor Pebbles! Maybe Ruddles will help sniff him out."

"Penelope's very upset," said Natty, turning for the gate. "So we're going to look really hard."

"She would be," said Mrs Plumley, looking concerned. "If Ruddles is a nuisance, you bring him back home."

"I will," said Natty with a wave.

She fastened Mrs Plumley's front gate and they continued on their way to the wood.

"I hope that dog doesn't turn out to be more trouble than he's worth," said Ned from his hiding place in the rucksack pocket. Natty hoped so too. Ruddles was such an eager little dog that already her arm felt as though it was being pulled from its socket.

They soon reached the end of the lane and took the path leading into the wood. It was silent beneath the trees, and the tracks that had been obvious on the lane were no longer so clear on the path, where the snow was spread more thinly, showing patches of bare earth.

"It's going to be harder than we thought to find him," said Natty.

"Maybe," said Ned. "But we'll do our best."

With these words he sprang from the rucksack pocket into the magic wind and stood before Natty and Ruddles a proper-sized pony, saddled and bridled and ready to go. Startled by the pony's sudden arrival, the little dog barked fiercely.

"That's enough, Ruddles. This is Ned. He's a very nice, very special pony."

Natty stroked Ned's warm chestnut neck and the pony leant forward, blowing steamy breath down his nostrils. Ruddles barked even louder.

"Stop it, Ruddles," said Natty

firmly. "If you keep on, I shall take you home."

"Give him a chance to get used to me," said Ned. "Let him off the lead. With luck he won't bark so much once he's loose."

Natty unclipped the lead and put it in her pocket. Then she took the reins and put her foot in the stirrup. The moment she touched the saddle her ordinary clothes disappeared and she was dressed in her magic riding clothes, which today included a long green riding mac to keep her warm and dry. Her rucksack turned into the usual saddlebags and hung across Ned's back. Ruddles whimpered with confusion.

"It's all right," said Natty. "It's still me."

The little dog gave a cautious wag of his tail and looked even more surprised when Ned said, "Come on, dog, use that nose and sniff out Pebbles." But he trotted on obediently without another bark, sometimes sniffing ahead, sometimes getting left behind and racing to catch up.

When Ned jumped the fallen log which lay across the path, Ruddles leapt it too, galloping alongside the pony as fast as his little legs would take him.

"I think he's got used to you," said Natty.

"Yes, he seems to be enjoying himself," said Ned. "He may turn out to be useful after all."

They settled down to a thorough search. Ned kept up a steady trot through the snow and when it got deep Ruddles bounded in great leaps. But whichever way they looked, there was no sign of a dappled grey pony in the long, empty stretches of wintery wood.

They slithered down a bank, sending a shower of snow and dead leaves before them, to arrive on the path that wound alongside the stream. The trees were thinner here, and they could see grey clouds hanging heavily above them, looking as if, at any minute, they would drop more snow. Ned blew clouds of steamy breath and for a moment he and Natty watched Ruddles dig energetically in the bank. Then the little dog stood still and cocked his head to one side, listening.

From further along the path came the sound of raised voices. Boys having an argument. Ruddles barked four times and put so much effort into it that each bark lifted him from the ground.

"That's enough," said Natty sharply.

But it was too late. Ruddles had given them away and the voices went silent. "I wonder who it is?" whispered Natty.

"Let's find out," said Ned. "Pick up the dog and put him inside your mac. We don't want him giving us away again."

Natty quickly dismounted and, keeping an arm linked through the reins so she didn't lose her magic riding clothes, she picked up the surprised Ruddles and stuffed him inside the front of her mac. He wriggled a bit, but she was firm and he stayed put. Then she swung herself back into the saddle. Ruddles seemed surprised to find himself on the pony but didn't bark again. He peeked from the mac and settled down to enjoy his ride.

"He looks quite comfortable," said Natty, patting his head, "for a dog that's never ridden before."

They rounded the bend in the path but there was no one there. Natty had at least expected to see someone disappearing between the trees.

"They're hiding," whispered Ned. "They've had no time to get away."

Without warning, a snowball

came flying through the air and landed with a smack on Ned's shoulder. The pony stood his ground and snorted.

"I can see you," shouted Natty. Underneath her mac, Ruddles growled and pushed his way out. Before she could stop him, he'd launched himself to the ground and, barking furiously, was running between the trees. He quickly flushed out not one but four shouting and protesting boys as he snapped at their heels. It was Smudger Evans and his gang.

Chapter 9
Clues

"Ruddles, come here at once!" ordered Natty, keeping her voice deep. "Leave the boys alone." She crossed her fingers, hoping her magic riding clothes disguise would work and the boys wouldn't recognize her voice.

Reluctantly the little dog came

and stood by Ned, a low growl rumbling in his throat, ready to attack again at the slightest provocation.

"Which stupid idiot threw a snowball at my pony?" said Natty. "You could have made him bolt."

"It wasn't meant to hit him. He got in the way," said Smudger.

"He threw it at me and missed," chimed in Henry. The skinny twins nodded in agreement.

"That's right. He threw it at him and missed," they echoed.

Natty didn't believe a word. The snowball had come from completely the wrong direction to hit Henry. But she didn't pursue it. It was enough that the boys didn't know who she was. Her magic riding clothes were amazing.

"What are you doing with that dog anyway?" Smudger asked. "We know him. It's that snappy little terrier that belongs to Mrs Plumley."

"He's helping me search for a pony. A dapple grey one called Pebbles. Have you seen him?"

Natty caught a momentary glint in Smudger's eyes before he turned his head away and addressed the gang.

"No, we ain't seen no pony, have we, lads?"

"No!"

All four of them shook their heads in exaggerated agreement.

"Because if you have, Penelope Potter would be glad to hear about it."

"Oh, it's Penelope Potter's pony, is it?" asked Smudger, turning wide, innocent eyes to Natty. "Poor Penelope. Fancy her losing her pony. That's a terrible thing to happen, isn't it, lads?"

If Natty hadn't been so keen to learn more, she would have burst out laughing. Smudger didn't mean a single word. As for the other three, nodding and looking solemn, it was a complete act.

"Well, now we know her pony's missing we can help look," said Smudger. "After all, a pony lost in the snow could starve to death."

Henry looked startled, as if he'd suddenly thought of something. "It could," he said. He looked wide-eyed at Smudger and added pointedly, "If it didn't have any food to eat!"

Smudger glared back. "Shut it, Henry!" He turned back to Natty. "If we see the pony, we'll let you know. Be nice to get it back for Penelope."

"Not for a reward or anything," piped up Henry, unable to help himself. For that he got a kick on the shin.

"If you see her, tell her we're keeping an eye out," said Smudger. "It's the least we can do."

He gave Henry an angry shove, and the four boys skirted the pony and the dog and carried on down the path.

Natty, Ned and Ruddles watched them go. The moment they were out of earshot, Natty exploded.

"It's them," she said. "All that pretence about being nice! They've taken Pebbles and hidden him somewhere. I'm certain of it."

"A good way of getting back at Penelope," nodded Ned.

"But there's more to it than that," said Natty. "When I heard them talking in the shed they wanted money. Lots of it. That's why I thought they were going to kidnap Penelope and hold her to ransom. But I think they've kidnapped Pebbles instead."

"Yes, but not for ransom. They're cleverer than that," said Ned. "Henry gave me the clue. If I'm right, they've taken Pebbles in the hope of Mr Potter offering a reward. If he does, my guess is they'll take

Pebbles home and claim it."

"The cheats!" fumed Natty. "That's dreadful. Of course Mr Potter will offer a reward. He'll want to get Pebbles back more than anything." Natty leaned eagerly over Ned's shoulder and looked at the ground. "If we follow their footprints and see where they came from, they could lead us straight to where Pebbles is hidden and we could rescue him."

"Good idea," said Ned. "We'll try it. Come on, Ruddles."

A confusing mass of churned snow and dead leaves led them in and out between the trees.

"The result of a snowball fight, I imagine," said Ned.

They followed the disturbed snow, bending round with the path, which took them at last to the narrow wooden bridge that crossed the stream. Here, the water flowed darkly beneath the snow-scuffed planks, but no one appeared to have crossed to the field on the other side. At the water's edge the snow was turned to slush, but only on this side of the bank.

"A dead end," said Natty, her spirits sinking. "It looks as though all they've been doing is mucking about and fighting as usual. That they've come this far and gone home again. If they have taken Pebbles, I can't think where they've put him."

"He's somewhere, Natty, and we must try to find out where."

It was a disappointed Natty who rode back along the path. All she could imagine was Pebbles locked away in a cold, lonely place.

"I hope they're feeding him properly. What does Smudger know about looking after ponies?"

"Not a lot, I imagine, which is why

we must find Pebbles as quickly as possible. He'll need plenty of hay to keep him warm in this weather."

"From the way Henry was talking, I don't think the gang had even thought of it," said Natty. "Poor Penelope. I bet she has, though."

The path turned away from the stream and went slowly uphill. Taking care not to slip, Ned trotted up the incline with Ruddles at his heels. The first flakes of a new fall of snow settled on Ned's mane and by the time they reached the edge of the wood it was snowing hard.

Natty dismounted and let go of

the reins. At once her magic riding clothes vanished and she was back in her jeans, anorak and woolly hat. She fumbled in her pocket with numb fingers for the dog lead. "Come here, Ruddles. Good boy." She clipped on the lead and took off her rucksack.

There was a whoosh of magic wind and the tiny Ned leapt from the snow into the front pocket. Ruddles sniffed at it curiously and Natty quickly pulled the rucksack on to her back, out of reach, before setting off along the lane.

"Oh, Natty, there you are!" said Jamie, looming out of the snow with Ben at his shoulder. "Where've you been? We've been looking for you for ages."

"Trying to find Pebbles, of course," Natty replied.

"We've looked too," said Ben.

"We went as far as the Ups and

Downs but no sign," added Jamie. "It's hard work trudging in this snow."

Ruddles pulled to go on. Natty wanted to tell them about meeting Smudger and the gang but it was impossible to work out how to explain it without mentioning Ned, and she couldn't do that.

"Look, I've got to take Ruddles back to Mrs Plumley and then I'm going to find out how Penelope is, and see if there's any news."

"You can't. Mum says you've got to come in now because it's snowing again and because of your flu."

"Oh, no!" said Natty. "Well, can you find out?"

"We've just seen Penelope," said Jamie.

"And she's really upset," added Ben. "The police have made it worse by saying that Pebbles is probably miles away by now."

"And there's a whopping reward," said Jamie. "Mr Potter's offering five hundred pounds for Pebbles's safe return!"

"Five hundred pounds!" Natty's jaw dropped in astonishment.

"He's going to print off posters on his computer and pin them up."

If Smudger had taken Pebbles, she couldn't allow him to claim five hundred pounds. Natty knew she must stop him somehow.

"Oh, and by the way," said Jamie, "what have you done with the toboggan?"

"I haven't done anything with it," said Natty. "It was by the back door where you left it."

"Well, it's not there now. So if you haven't taken it, who has?"

Chapter 10
The Plot Thickens

As Natty walked down Mrs Plumley's path after delivering Ruddles home, she had a lot to think about. She would have liked to have gone in and had the warming cup of cocoa Mrs Plumley offered, but thought she'd better ask Mum first. So, with head bent against the snow, she went in the side gate and round to the back door. Jamie was right, the toboggan had gone.

"Mum," she called, poking her head round the door and dropping snowflakes all over the mat, "can I have cocoa at Mrs Plumley's?"

"Shout any louder and the whole world'll hear you," said Jamie, who was in the kitchen making toast. Ben, with hands over his ears, pulled a face. Natty poked her tongue out at both of them.

"That's fine," said Mum, coming to the door. "But I don't want you

162

out in this snowstorm. You'll be back in bed if you're not careful."

"Thanks, Mum."

Natty was gone before Mum had time to change her mind. She was about to open Mrs Plumley's gate when a blast of magic wind sent the snowflakes whirling. Ned stood beside her and gave her a nudge.

"Hop up," he said. "Before you go for your cocoa I think we ought to find out what's going on."

"With the toboggan, you mean?"

"With Smudger's gang. We'll go to the shed like you did before. We may be lucky and pick up some useful information."

"Just so long as Mum doesn't find out," said Natty, swinging herself into the saddle. At once she was wearing her magic riding clothes with the green riding mac on top. The peak on her hat kept the icy flakes from her face, and she trusted Ned's four steady legs to see them safely through the snow.

Head lowered to the wind, the pony stepped out purposefully. Trudging through the ever-thickening drifts, they passed Penelope's deserted stable yard and headed for the main road and the lane that led to the allotments. In spite of the thickly falling flakes, Natty was toasty warm in her mac, and Ned didn't appear to notice the cold either. He shook the snow from his forelock and plodded on.

It wasn't long before they reached the gap in the hedge where Natty and the boys had got in to the allotments last time.

"The gap's too small for me," said Ned.

"There's a gate further on," Natty replied, but when they got to it and shook the snow from the chain, they found it fastened with a padlock.

"We'll jump," said Ned.

"But you could go in the rucksack," said Natty.

"There's no need. Just hold on tight. Think of showjumping under the bed. It's just the same."

"Except for the snow," replied Natty.

Ned marched in a circle, then cantered three straight strides towards the gate and took off. Pony and rider soared through the air, landing safely on the other side. Natty grinned with relief. It was scary jumping in the snow.

Ned skirted the vegetable plots, keeping close to the hedge.

"There's the shed," said Natty, pointing it out. The black sides showed up starkly under the roof's thick snow covering.

"Then it's time for you to carry me."

Natty sprang from Ned's back. She was sorry to lose her riding mac. Her anorak was not nearly so warm. She held the rucksack ready and the magic wind blew. Ned was inside the front pocket in a jiffy. Natty took a deep breath, held the rucksack in front of her so Ned could see where they were going, and set off across the open ground. The snow made the uneven earth seem smooth and she stumbled several times, but eventually made it to the back of the shed, her heart thudding against her ribs.

The shed appeared deserted.

Cautiously, she peeped through the window but could see nothing.

"Go round to the entrance," said Ned. "We'll take a look inside."

Snow had drifted up against the door and it was clear that no one had opened it for a while.

"But if I go in they'll know by my footprints."

"We can't worry about that, Natty. We need information."

Reluctantly Natty lifted the latch, expecting the shed to be locked. It wasn't and she was able to push the door open. She went quickly inside, closing it behind her. There was not much to see: an old table, a broken wheelbarrow and Smudger's bike minus its front wheel. The buckled wheel was lying across a pile of old boxes. Three strings of onions hung from the roof and there were some beansticks propped in a corner.

"Hardly worth coming in for," said Natty.

"Agreed," said Ned. Natty was about to let them out again when her hand froze on the latch. There were voices outside and one of them was Smudger's.

She looked for somewhere to hide

and was stopped by a blast of magic wind. The big Ned filled the shed, knocking a string of onions to the floor.

"Get on," he said, bending down on one knee to make room.

"Hey, look Smudge, fresh footprints." It was Henry right outside the door.

Natty grabbed a handful of mane and jumped for the saddle. Two things happened at once. The magic wind blew and Smudger came in. Natty glimpsed his angry face high above her as Ned galloped underneath the wheelbarrow.

"There's no one in here." That was Henry.

"Hey, Smudge, can we bring the toboggan in? It's freezing out here."

"Yeah, bring it in quick and shut the door."

There were some grunts and a bump as something heavy was leant against the shed wall and the door was shut.

"Someone's been having a poke around," said Stew, watching Smudger pick up the string of onions and put it thoughtfully on the table.

"Jamie Deakin and his sidekick,"

said Nick. "Lucky we hadn't already got the toboggan here."

"Shut it!" snapped Smudger. Giant boots passed the wheelbarrow, thudding against the earth. They halted and in the silence that followed, Natty's nose tickled.

"Atishoo!" She had sneezed before she could stop it. Ned quickly backed into a broken flower pot lying on its side. He was just in time. Through a crack, Natty could see Smudger's face peering under the wheelbarrow. She held her breath.

"What is it, Smudge?" Henry asked.

"Check behind the boxes. I'm sure I heard something."

"Probably a rat," said Stew.

"Huh! As long as it's not a Deakin rat," muttered Smudger.

"There's no one in here," said Nick. "Couldn't be. There's nowhere for a person to hide."

"No, you're right," said Smudger. "Still, now we got the toboggan we'll make sure we get that out of sight. Your job, Henry. Cover it."

"Right-o, Smudge."

There was a bumping of boxes being moved, a scraping as the toboggan slid over and more scuffling.

"All right, all right, Henry, that's enough." Smudger waited for silence. "Now that we got the toboggan, what we got to do is easy enough – but we don't want any mistakes. This is the plan so listen carefully."

Chapter 11
A Long Wait Till Midnight

Crouching low on Ned's back, her head almost touching the flower pot, Natty hardly dared breathe. She was shaking with a mixture of indignation and fear. Indignation that the gang had stolen their toboggan, and fear in case she and Ned should be discovered.

"Lucky, I got lucky," crowed Henry. "I was going to let Jamie Deakin's tyres down till I saw the toboggan."

"Cool," said Nick.

"No need to overdo the congratulations. I said listen. We meet back here at midnight."

"Midnight, Smudge?" Henry wailed. "I'll never get out that late two nights in a row."

"You better had. Down the drainpipe if necessary. Bring a torch. We take the toboggan and go from here to the Potters' barn. There we collect a bale of hay. Which is why we do it in the dead of night, see, Henry? So we don't get caught."

"We should have thought about feeding the nag before," said Stew.

"Well, we've thought about it now," said Smudger. "We ferry the hay out on the toboggan and on the way back Henry dumps it back where it came from."

"No, Smudge, can't we keep it?"

"It's evidence against us. We get rid of it." Henry groaned, but Smudger ignored him.

"Do we know if there's a reward yet?" asked Nick.

"There's a notice just gone up in the shop window," said Smudger.

"Five hundred pounds for the return of Penelope Potter's stolen pony."

"Five hundred!" repeated Stew.

"We could fetch him now," said Henry.

"Too soon," said Smudger. "It'd look suspicious, what with the notice only just going up. Anyway, the longer we leave it, the more grateful they'll be. We'll bring him back tomorrow afternoon, claim the reward then and, hey presto, I get a brand-new bike."

"Neat, Smudge," said Nick. "But about tonight. Do we still go if it's snowing?"

"Course we do. We can't let the animal starve. We got to get it back in one piece, otherwise no reward. Any questions?" There were none. "OK, men. Rendezvous back here at midnight. Don't be late."

Natty was relieved to hear the shed door open and the boys tumble out laughing before it was closed again. Ned waited until their voices faded before he moved.

"That's terrible, Ned," said Natty. "They've taken Pebbles and not even thought to feed him. He'll be so hungry. And all Smudger cares about is the reward."

"It's our chance to find him, Natty. We'll be at the stable yard waiting, and when they take the hay, we'll follow them."

"Yes, and steal him back again."

"That's our plan," said Ned. "Now we must get you to Mrs Plumley's house for that cup of cocoa."

Ned stepped out from the broken flower pot and trotted into the middle of the shed.

"Don't get off," he said. "Duck!"

The magic wind blew and Natty crouched low to avoid hitting the roof. Ned unlatched the door with his teeth and pulled it

181

open. Snowflakes whirled in their faces. The pony looked both ways and stepped outside. Natty pulled the door closed behind them and Ned ploughed his way across the blanketed allotments to the gate.

By the time they were making their way up the lane towards home, Natty was wondering if the snow would ever stop. Just before they reached Penelope's stable yard, she slid from Ned's back.

"I'd better carry you from here," she said, letting go of the reins and saying a silent goodbye to her magic riding clothes.

"Good idea," said Ned, and he was back in the rucksack pocket almost before Natty had time to blink. She shivered, pulled the rucksack on to her back and plodded on through the freezing snow.

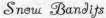

"Natty, wait!"

The voice was unexpected and made her jump. She turned round to see Penelope coming out from the stable yard, muffled up against the cold, her face a picture of misery, peering out from beneath a furry hood.

"I came to see if Pebbles had come home." Penelope's bottom lip trembled. "But I think he's gone for ever."

"No, not for ever," said Natty. "I'm certain you'll get him back."

"I wish I was certain," said Penelope. "He could be anywhere, freezing to death in the snow."

Natty didn't know what to say. It was hard knowing that Smudger and the gang had Pebbles locked up somewhere and that, even if the pony was hungry, he was safe.

"Don't worry," she said, putting her arm round Penelope's shoulder. "I'm sure he'll be back by tomorrow."

"Don't be stupid, you can't possibly know that," said Penelope, pushing Natty's arm away. "Daddy said he'd get me another pony. But I don't want another pony. I want Pebbles." And, sobbing, she stumbled off in the direction of her house. Natty started after her.

"No," said Ned. "Let her go."

"But couldn't I tell her about Smudger? Make her promise not to say anything until tomorrow?"

"Penelope mustn't know a thing, Natty. She won't keep it a secret. You know what's she's like. And if the gang become suspicious or she accuses them, we mightn't find out where Pebbles is for days."

Natty sighed. She could see that Ned was right. She trudged on towards Mrs Plumley's gate and her cup of cocoa, more determined than ever that Pebbles should be rescued as soon as possible.

It was a long time to wait until midnight and Natty thought the hours would never pass. Bedtime came at last, and when Mum tucked her up, Ned watched from the safety of his poster while Tabitha curled up in her usual place on Natty's feet, purring. Ned had promised to wake her, so she didn't set her alarm clock.

It took ages to get to sleep, but when she did it seemed her eyes had only been closed for five minutes before she felt a nuzzle on her arm and warm breath on her face, and heard a whispered "Wake up!" in her ear.

Tabitha hardly stirred when Natty sat up and took her torch from under the pillow. She switched it on to find the big Ned filling the space beside the bed, but only for a moment. He magicked himself tiny and jumped into the rucksack pocket, ready to go. It was cold and Natty quickly pulled on her waiting clothes, including her thermal vest and an extra pair of socks, before peeping out of the window.

The snow had stopped and the sky was full of stars. A round moon shone a silvery glow on an icy world.

"It's so light," said Natty, in wonder.

"And very cold," said Ned. "Don't forget; hat, scarf and gloves."

Natty picked up the rucksack and began a careful creep downstairs. By the time she reached the back door she was wrapped up warmly. She shone her torch on the kitchen clock. Five minutes to midnight. She pulled on her boots and quietly let herself out. Crunching through the frosted snow, she went round to the side gate, her breath turning to smoky clouds in the icy air.

"It's so light, I don't need the torch," she whispered.

"Which means you must take care not to be seen," said Ned.

"Don't worry, I will."

Keeping in the shelter of the hedge, Natty looked up at the house. All the windows were dark, and the bare branches of the fig tree made shadows on the wall. It was so still, it was as if the night were holding its breath. She looked down the lane. About now, Smudger and his gang would be arriving at the shed to collect the toboggan. She hurried on

so as to be hidden and waiting when they reached the stable yard.

She found the yard gate and Pebbles's stable door open as if both were waiting for the pony's return. Well, with Ned's help he would be back soon. There was no sign of the gang yet and the stable looked like the best place to hide. Natty stood in the doorway and checked the yard entrance. It was a horrible shock when a hand clamped itself across her mouth and she was pulled backwards into the stable.

She gasped, twisted and struggled.

"Shush, Natty, stop it! It's me!"

The hand was taken away.

"Penelope! What are you doing here at this time of night?"

"I was about to ask you the very same question," came the reply.

Chapter 12
Stalking the Bandits

There was nothing for it. Natty would have to tell Penelope exactly why she was there. The boys would be turning up to take the hay at any minute.

"OK," said Natty. "There's not much time, so listen carefully. Smudger Evans and the gang have taken Pebbles."

"What?"

"Smudger guessed your dad would offer a reward if Pebbles was stolen. Their plan is to bring him back, pretend they found him, and claim it."

"I'll chop them up and boil them in oil for this," said Penelope.

"Don't get too angry, because they'll be here any minute and they mustn't see us."

"What do you mean mustn't see us? I'm going to pulverize them."

"No! They're going to take a bale of hay as feed for Pebbles. It's our chance to find out exactly where he's being hidden."

"How do you know all this?" asked Penelope.

"I overheard them talking about it."

"I wish you'd told me before. I'd have forced them to tell me where he is."

"They'd have denied it," said Natty. "Think what they're like. This way we'll get Pebbles back in no time."

"And save the reward money," said Penelope. "They're not getting a penny."

"I should hope not. But you see why we mustn't give ourselves away?" said Natty. "The most important thing is to rescue Pebbles."

"Of course," said Penelope. "When I couldn't sleep I came to the stable to wish him back and it's nearly worked. It's almost my complete wish."

"Nearly but not quite," said Natty with a grin. "Shush, I can hear something."

While Penelope peered round the corner of the stable door, Natty took off her rucksack to check Ned was all right. He nodded encouragingly at her from the front pocket. It was more difficult now Penelope was with them, and worrying because Penelope's short temper might give them away.

Natty pulled on the rucksack and joined Penelope in time to watch four creeping figures slink into the yard towing a toboggan. It was easy to see it was Smudger and the gang. They stood in a pool of moonlight by the barn door and slowly pulled it open. The skinny twins went inside and a few seconds later came out dragging a bale of hay, which the others helped load on to the toboggan.

Penelope was rigid with fury, and Natty put a restraining hand on her arm as the boys towed the hay out of the yard and, with the occasional flash of a torch, set off along the lane in the direction of Winchway Wood.

"We'll give them a start and then follow, making sure they don't see us."

"Don't worry. I won't give us away," said Penelope. "Not till I'm good and ready."

The two girls set off, with Natty hoping that Penelope wouldn't do anything foolish. They could see the boys at the end of the lane, about to disappear into the dark of the woods. So far so good.

"Come on," whispered Natty. "We don't want to lose them."

She need not have worried. The toboggan runners left an easy trail to follow in the moonlight.

"I hope it's not far," grumbled Penelope. "It's hard work walking in snow."

Natty didn't reply but kept up a steady plod. Of course, Penelope was right. Turning a bend where the path dropped down towards the stream, they had to stop and take shelter amongst the trees. The boys had met with an accident and were struggling to put the hay bale back on the toboggan. Now they were in the woods there was no caution about noise and Smudger's voice was raised in fury.

"Henry, you clumsy lump!" he raged.

"It wasn't my fault. I slipped. Anyone could have done the same."

"But it wasn't anyone. It was you, as usual."

"No harm done," said Stew, when the bale was back on the toboggan.

"Think of the reward," said Nick.

"Yeah, five hundred pounds," said Henry. "Plenty for a new bike."

"Yeah," said Smudger, and rubbed his hands together. "And if you hadn't forgotten about horse food it would have been dead easy. The nag could have carried his own hay. All we need have done was fetch it back and claim the reward."

"Why's it my fault we didn't think about horse food?"

"'Cos you, Henry, said you knew about looking after horses."

"I never did. I said if Penelope Potter could look after a horse then it must be easy. That's what I said."

It was all Natty could do to stop Penelope from rushing forward.

"No," she whispered. "Don't let them get to you. Think of finding Pebbles."

"I hate them," said Penelope, her voice low but furious. "Hate them, hate them, hate them."

Natty hung on to her arm and wouldn't let go. Pulling Penelope behind a tree, she made her wait until the boys had moved on.

"Honestly, Natty, they could have let Pebbles starve to death, they're so thick."

"He'll certainly be hungry, but when we've found him we can take him home and look after him properly," said Natty, checking to see if the coast was clear. "Come on."

The boys never once looked back, but even if they had, the two girls were ready to dart for cover. Each step they took brought them closer to the captive pony. It made Natty feel positively cheerful and she glowed with warmth underneath her woolly hat as they crunched through the crisp snow.

When the boys reached the narrow wooden bridge spanning the stream, they stopped and seemed uncertain. Natty signalled to Penelope that they should get closer. Creeping from tree to tree, the girls came within earshot.

"The bale's too heavy to carry upstream," Henry said, his voice clear in the crisp cold air. "We'll have to keep it on the toboggan, cross the bridge and go round that way."

"I don't like the idea of leaving tracks," said Smudger, kicking at some ice already formed at the water's edge. "They'll be a dead giveaway. So far we've always gone up by the water."

Stew pointed to the sky, where heavy clouds were gathering, blotting out the stars. "Looks like more snow coming. Tracks are the least of our worries."

"Yeah," said Nick. "We need to feed the nag some hay. The quicker we do that, the quicker we can get home to our beds."

"And anyway," said Henry reasonably, "tomorrow we're going to fetch it home and collect the reward."

"Right, we'll take a chance and go across the bridge," said Smudger, giving in. "Pull away, Henry. Us others will get behind and push."

Only it was Henry who pulled, and Nick and Stew who pushed. There wasn't room for Smudger as well. He strolled over behind them.

"Wherever have they hidden him?" wondered Penelope.

"I guessed it was somewhere nearby," said Natty. "I saw them near here yesterday. They must have made Pebbles walk up the stream to hide his footprints."

Once the boys were across the bridge they hugged the riverbank on the far side. Natty and Penelope quickly followed them over. The gang, dark shapes against the white of the snow, appeared to be making for a small spinney further upstream. There was no cover for the girls now and they waited until the boys disappeared amongst the trees. Then they set off as fast as they could to catch up.

Although the sky was clouding over, there was still occasional moonlight to show up the toboggan tracks, and they followed them into the trees until they came into a clearing where there was an old wooden hut.

The boys fumbled with a long piece of wood propped across the door. From inside came restless thuds and a harsh snorting.

"Keep your hair on, matey," said Smudger. "We've got you a whole bale of hay."

Henry pulled the door open a crack. Hooves kicked back against the wood and there was a loud, anxious whinny from a crazed and lonely pony.

"Pebbles!" cried Penelope, and before Natty could stop her, she raced towards the shed and the startled boys.

Chapter 13
Ned to the Rescue

Everything happened at once. The shed door burst open and Pebbles barged out, pushing between Henry and Stew, who both tried to grab the broken halter rope the pony was trailing. Smudger and Nick put their efforts into fending off the advancing Penelope, who dodged them only to catch her foot in the toboggan rope. She yelped with pain and landed in an uncomfortable heap.

Pebbles reared up to avoid the grasping hands, jumped the hay bale and galloped off into the night. Dismayed, Natty ran forward to help Penelope, who lay groaning in the snow.

"How did you two get here?" cried the confused and furious Smudger.

"Penelope, are you all right?" Natty asked, kneeling down beside her.

"It's my ankle. I think it's broken."

The four boys looked down with pale faces and dark eyes at the two girls in the snow.

"We'll get help," said Henry, backing off.

"And get the pony back," said Smudger. "We found him on information received. So we'll be expecting the reward."

"So that's why you were bringing a bale of hay here on our toboggan, is it?" said Natty. "You didn't find him, you stole him." Smudger opened his mouth to reply, but nothing came out. "Penelope, can you move your ankle?" asked Natty, turning her attention back to what really mattered.

"No, it's agony."

"Tell the Potters," said Natty to the boys. "Get help like Henry says. That's what you must do."

"Yes," nodded Nick and Stew together, with serious expressions.

"Come on, Smudger," called Henry, already on his way. "We got to capture the pony."

Smudger backed away a few steps, then turned and stumbled after Henry and the twins.

"My pony's lost, my ankle hurts like anything, and I'm freezing," said Penelope. "This isn't what I wished at all." And she moaned in despair.

"Don't worry," said Natty. "We'll get you home and if Pebbles has got any sense, that's where he's gone too. Just stay there for a minute while I sort things out."

Natty quickly put the rucksack on top of the hay bale and took off her anorak, covering Penelope with it for extra warmth. The toboggan

was the answer, she could see that.
If she could get Penelope on to it,
she could be pulled home.

The moon disappeared behind a
mass of dark cloud and, with the
stirring of an icy wind, the trees shed
snow. The night was closing in. The
tiny Ned trotted across the hay bale.

"Be quick, Natty," he whispered.
"We can't wait here. It's too cold and
more snow's coming. Get Penelope
on to the toboggan as fast as you can.
Keep hold of the rope and get on
me. After that I can do the pulling."

"But what if Penelope sees you?
I should have made the boys wait.

They could have pulled her."

"Don't worry, she won't see me. I'll make sure of that. The sooner her ankle's looked at the better."

"Do you think the boys will find Pebbles?"

"He'll have gone home," said Ned. "I'm certain of it. He'll be tucked up in his stable by the time we get back."

Ned jumped from the hay bale, a miniature pony trotting lightly across the frosted snow. Natty took out her torch and pulled on her rucksack. It was intensely dark now, and the air felt muffled. She pushed the bale of hay from the toboggan and it rolled off and fell apart. Taking advantage of the hay flaps, Natty laid a row along the wooden slats before pushing the toboggan alongside Penelope's huddled figure.

"Right," said Natty. "On to the toboggan with you, then we can get you home."

She tried lifting Penelope but she was too heavy and did nothing but groan.

"You've got to help me," said Natty. "Sit up so I can get my arms under you. Hop with your good leg."

"I can't!"

"You must. You've got to. The toboggan'll be much warmer than the snow. It's got a hay mattress on it. Now come on. Try."

Eventually, after much heaving on Natty's part, Penelope pushed off with her good leg and Natty got her bottom on to the toboggan. Carefully guiding the hurt leg into place, Natty covered all of Penelope with a layer of hay, tucking the anorak over the top.

"I'll never walk again," Penelope moaned. "I wish I was in bed."

Natty put a pillow of hay under Penelope's head before pulling off

her own woolly hat and squashing it
over the one Penelope was already
wearing, making sure it came well
down over her ears and her eyes.

There was a blast of magic wind
and the big Ned stood, tacked up
and ready, in front of the toboggan.

"Pull carefully," said Penelope, weakly. "Otherwise I might roll off."

"I will," promised Natty, picking up the rope.

It was too short, and she wondered how she was going to get on Ned and keep hold of it at the same time. Ned helped by manoeuvring himself sideways and holding the torch in his teeth. It was awkward until Natty's seat touched the saddle, but when her magic riding clothes appeared, everything changed. The toboggan turned into a sleigh, with Ned attached to it by a proper harness, while Penelope was safely tucked up under a pile of blankets. They were ready to go.

"Brilliant," whispered Natty, taking back the torch.

"And Penelope won't notice a thing," said Ned. "Because she's fast asleep. I've made sure of that." Natty grinned. Ned's magic was truly amazing. She shone the torch to light their way just as the first snowflakes fell. "But we must be quick," the pony said, "otherwise we'll all end up like snowmen." He set off at a brisk trot between the trees, with the sleigh gliding across the snow behind him.

By the time they reached the narrow bridge, the wind was blowing in gusts, whipping the snow into spirals and swirls, beating it into their faces. Natty bent double over Ned's neck and did her best to guide them with the torch. The pony trod the boards carefully. The bridge was just wide enough for the sleigh to cross, but he couldn't afford to slip; and the snow was blinding. One cautious step followed another until, at last, the pony and the sleigh were finally over.

"This is no good," cried Ned above the wind. "We can't stay out in this blizzard."

He was right. Even wearing the big riding mac, Natty was beginning to freeze. They needed to find shelter.

"We'll go home a different way," Ned cried, turning off the path and trotting ahead.

Natty couldn't think where they were going. She shone the torch as best she could, but against the blizzard its light was feeble. How glad she was to be with Ned! But even with a magic pony, she couldn't think how they would get home safely.

Chapter 14
Not Over the Hill but Under

To Natty's surprise, Ned appeared
to be trotting straight towards an
unclimbable bank. It loomed up in
front of them, and when he didn't
turn away, she ducked, expecting a
crash. But the crash didn't happen.
Instead a violent gust of wind picked
them up and spun them away. The

surprise of it sent her heart racing until she realized it was Ned's magic wind and not the storm. Then, when the wind faded, they were no longer out in the blizzard but somewhere dark and still.

"Ned, where are we?" she asked, shining her torch into the passageway that lay ahead.

"In an old badger set."

"Then we're tiny!"

"We are indeed. But there are no badgers to worry about." Ned twitched his nostrils. "This set has been taken over by rabbits."

Natty looked behind her. Penelope

was still tucked up, fast asleep, but the sleigh had gone. In its place was a four-wheeled carriage, perfect for travelling along the earth floor of the tunnel.

"Point the torch ahead," said Ned. "Provided that I don't take a wrong turning, we should come out at the beginning of the wood. Hold tight and off we go."

Ned set off at a trot, with the carriage wheeling along behind him. He broke into a canter. Unable to see far ahead and travelling at what appeared to be reckless speed, they raced through the long dark tunnel, which Natty found alarming. But she kept the torch beam as steady as she could and clung on.

It no longer felt so cold and when they came into a large cavern, Natty realized why. It was filled with huge furry bundles and the sound of steady breathing. The torch picked out a giant paw here and a twitching nose there, and after Natty counted six white bobtails, it was obvious it was a family of rabbits huddled together for warmth and comfort. Ned wove carefully around the sleeping bunnies but Natty was still afraid they might wake up. It wasn't until pony and carriage were through the cavern and heading uphill along another tunnel that she let out a sigh of relief. The rabbits hadn't noticed a thing.

Higher and higher they climbed, until the temperature started to drop again and Natty guessed they must be nearing the open air once more. She was beginning to think that the worst was over and that soon they would be home when the ground became uneven. Ned slowed to a walk in order to steer the carriage round several large clods of earth which lay scattered in their path. In the end they were forced to a stop in front of a huge mound.

"Looks like the roof has fallen in," said Ned. "I'm not sure we can get by."

"But we must," said Natty. "We can't go back. There's no room to turn the carriage."

Natty shone her torch over the fallen earth until it lit up a kind of tunnel lay-by that appeared lower and narrower than the main tunnel, but was a possible way round.

"Ned, could we squeeze through there?"

"We might just manage it," replied the pony. "You'll have to make sure the gap's big enough and that it's not a dead end. Pull a hair from my mane and wrap it round one of your fingers so you can let go of the reins. Remember, the hair will keep you small."

Natty took off her gloves and shoved them in her mac pocket. Taking hold of a hair, she pulled. It was full of spring and it took a few moments of tricky wrapping before she had it wound around her finger. She held it firmly in place.

Taking a deep breath, she swung herself to the ground and, imagining the worst, let go of the reins. She stayed tiny and, laughing with relief, shone the torch ahead. She stepped cautiously into the lay-by area, following it round until she felt a cold breeze on her face and realized she had come back into the main tunnel. She hurried to tell Ned.

"What do you think?" he asked, champing at the bit.

"You should be able to get the carriage through," said Natty. "The roof's low but I'm sure it's wide enough, and I think we're nearly at the end of the tunnel."

"Right," he said. "You shine the way and I'll follow."

Ned lowered his head to avoid hitting the roof, and came slowly forward. It was a tight turn but the pony angled it perfectly, and the carriage was wheeling round the bend nicely when it came to a sudden juddering stop and wouldn't budge.

"Now what?" asked Ned. He couldn't turn to look himself; he didn't have room.

"I'll go back," said Natty. The only way she could do this was by getting down on her hands and knees and crawling underneath the carriage. "I can see what it is," she called. "The wheel's hit a boulder. It's too heavy to move, but if I push and you pull, the wheel might lift over."

"We'll give it a try," called Ned.

"Are you ready?" Natty quickly crawled out at the back of the carriage and leaned against it.

"Ready."

"One, two, three – heave!"

The carriage creaked as Ned strained to pull and Natty to push.

Slowly the wheel lifted up, up and over the boulder, coming down with a jarring bump. Natty was squeezing round the side of the carriage to get back on Ned when the sound of a sleepy voice made her stop.

"What's up? Where am I?" It was Penelope. She had woken up.

"You're nearly home," Natty whispered soothingly. "Not much further to go."

"Why aren't I in bed?" asked the sleepy voice.

"You are, sort of," said Natty. "Go back to sleep."

Penelope didn't say anything else,

which was a relief, and Natty hurried to Ned's side, swinging herself on to his back and letting go of the chestnut hair the moment she took up the reins.

"No time to waste," Ned whispered. "The sleeping magic's wearing off." And he set off at a brisk trot. Soon the wind was whistling and a swirl of snowflakes the size of frozen pancakes blew into the tunnel, forcing Natty to duck. Ignoring them, Ned cantered into a draught of magic wind.

It was snowing even harder and was difficult to see. Natty knew they were big again, but had no idea where they were. The carriage had gone, and once again Ned was pulling the sleigh, skilfully steering it between the trees towards what Natty hoped was the edge of the wood.

Through the howl of the wind she caught a snatch of calling and a shrill whistle.

"It's Jamie, your mum and dad, and Mr Potter," said Ned.

"Over here!" cried Natty, calling back.

She dismounted quickly and Ned's magic wind blew one last time, taking her riding clothes, the sleigh and Ned away with it. In her hand she held the toboggan rope, and on the toboggan Penelope struggled to sit up.

"Where am I?" she cried. "I thought I was at home in bed."

"You will be soon," said Natty. "Don't move. You've got a bad ankle, don't forget."

"Keep going, Natty!" It was Ned's voice coming from her rucksack. "Head straight for the lights."

Glad that Ned was still guiding her, Natty pulled on the toboggan rope and trudged forward. Torchlight flickered and was gone. Then it flickered again between the flurries of snowflakes ahead.

"We're here," she called again. "We're over here."

From behind her came three ear-splitting blasts of the referee whistle. Penelope had remembered the help signal.

Chapter 15
Home at Last

"Faster!" Penelope cried. "They're calling us."

"I'm doing my best," panted Natty, stumbling over a hidden tree root.

"We're over here," cried Penelope but the wind, for all her effort, whipped and buffeted her voice into nothing. She gave three more whistle blasts.

That did the trick, for suddenly there was torchlight everywhere, and faces and smiles, and Mum hugging Natty, and someone taking the toboggan rope, and Mr Potter scooping Penelope into his arms.

"Mind my ankle," she said, but being lifted didn't stop her from clasping her father about the neck and holding on tight.

Then Mr Potter told them Pebbles was safe – and thank goodness for Henry Henforth, who had woken him up.

Natty sighed with relief, burying her face in her mum's jacket. Apart from Penelope's hurt ankle, everything was all right.

"Whatever made you go out in the middle of the night?" Dad asked. "And in a blizzard. How could you be so foolish?"

"There wasn't a blizzard when we started," Natty replied. "And we had to rescue Pebbles."

"And the toboggan," said Jamie, glad to see it back.

"Let's get them home," said Mum. "They can explain all about it later."

Natty was suddenly very tired.

It was all she could do to put one foot in front of the other. But, with Dad's arm round her, she managed the walk home.

When they got to the garden gate, Dad went on with Mr Potter to help look after Penelope and Mum and Jamie took Natty indoors.

"Bed," said Mum, pulling off the rucksack and anorak. "Straight away. You can explain exactly what happened in the morning."

"I can't wait to hear," added Jamie, smiling sleepily.

Natty carried her rucksack upstairs and put it on the chest of drawers underneath Ned's poster. The tiny pony jumped from the front pocket and trotted towards her.

"Well done, Natty. Mission accomplished," he said. "It was quite an adventure."

"It was," said Natty. "Thank you, Ned. I'd never ever have got Penelope home without you."

"Don't mention it," said the pony. "I hope that in the morning you can explain what happened to everyone's satisfaction." And with a leap he jumped into his poster and became a picture again.

"Natty, love, aren't you undressed

yet?" asked Mum coming in. "Clothes off, pyjamas on, and into bed with you."

It was very late when Natty woke the next morning. Ned looked down from his pony poster and she waved a cheery hello. Outside, the snow had stopped. She remembered what Ned had said about explaining everything, and as she went downstairs she thought how best to do it. She needn't have worried. Mum and Jamie already knew what had happened. Dad had heard it from Penelope last night.

"What I can't understand," said

Mum, "is how you managed to pull the toboggan so far in that blizzard. But thank goodness you did."

"Is Penelope's ankle all right?" Natty asked, quickly changing the subject.

"Not broken. Just badly sprained," said Mum. "She wants you and Jamie to go round and see her this morning."

"I'll help look after Pebbles," said Natty. "And take him some carrots. Poor pony. He must have had a horrid time locked in that shed."

"I think there's going to be quite a crowd of you looking after Pebbles," said Mum with a smile, and went into the kitchen to make toast.

"What does she mean?"

Jamie's face spread into the broadest of grins and his eyes twinkled.

"Smudger and the others have had the biggest telling-off ever, and they've got to do chores for Mr Potter every day of the Christmas holidays to make up."

Natty's eyes opened wide.

"Really? Penelope'll love that."

"I'm going to show her my rope trick to cheer her up. At least with a sprained ankle she won't keep on about being my assistant at the Christmas Show."

"I wouldn't bet on it," said Natty.

She was right. Apart from hello, it was the first thing Penelope said when Mrs Potter showed Jamie and Natty into the living room, where she was sitting with her bandaged ankle propped up on a stool.

"It's only a sprain, Jamie. I'll be better in time for the Christmas Show."

"We'll have to wait and see," said Mrs Potter, pursing her lips and leaving them to it. Obviously, she didn't agree.

Penelope fixed a dazzling smile on Jamie, making him uncomfortable, Natty could tell. But, rallying round, he put on his magician's hat and cloak, and spread his arms wide.

"*Ladies. For your delight, allow me to present my famous Indian rope trick.*" Penelope applauded. Jamie bowed his thanks and took off his top hat. From inside the hat he took out a piece of rope. "*For this special and amazing trick I need a volunteer from the audience to assist me.*"

"I volunteer," cried Penelope, putting up her hand. "What do I have to do?"

"*Please inspect this piece of rope.*" With a bow Jamie gave the rope to Penelope, who crumpled and twisted and pulled it.

"It looks like an ordinary rope to me," she said.

"*Indeed, that is all it is!*"

With a flourish, Jamie dropped the rope back into the hat, tapped the hat with his magic wand, and said:

"*Ropus diddle pocus,*

Dee diddle hocus dee."

He replaced the hat on his head and Natty crossed her fingers. Slowly the hat lifted and the rope pushed it higher and higher until it balanced way above Jamie's head. It was most impressive. Then, with a twirl of his cloak, the rope collapsed, and Jamie caught the hat and bowed. He grinned with pleasure. The trick had worked.

Both Natty and Penelope applauded vigorously.

"Brilliant," said Natty.

"And for my next trick…" said Jamie, tossing his hat and catching it. "No, only joking."

"Yes, please do it again," pleaded Penelope. "It was so good."

Jamie was saved from having to do so by the door opening and Mr Potter coming in.

"Ah, Natty, just the person I want to see," he said, "to thank you for your splendid detective work and for bringing Penelope home safely." Natty blushed deeply. "And, as you know, there is a reward for information leading to the return of

Pebbles. Well, here it is, and richly deserved." He held out a bulky white envelope. Natty's jaw dropped and she stared at it, then looked up at Mr Potter wonderingly.

"But I didn't do it for the reward," she said.

"I know," said Mr Potter. "Which is why it's such a pleasure to give it to you. I've discussed it with your dad. It's for finding Pebbles and for bravely saving my Penny Wenny Pops."

Mr Potter thrust the envelope into Natty's hand, and suddenly Jamie was thumping her on the back.

"Congratulations, little sister," he beamed.

Natty didn't know what to say and mumbled a thank you. She had never thought of earning the reward for herself. It was most unexpected.

"And you'll have to exercise Pebbles for me," said Penelope. "Someone's got to ride him while I can't."

"Well," said Natty with a shy smile, "this makes up for spending the first three days of the school holidays in bed with flu." Which was exactly what she told Ned when she arrived home later.

"Now I can buy the Christmas presents of my dreams. The Vanishing Box Trick from Mr Cosby for Jamie, a new knitting machine for Mum, and an electric screwdriver for Dad. He said it was a luxury he couldn't afford, but I can, and he's been wanting one for ages."

She looked up at Ned with shining eyes. Her magic pony's present was to be a bumper bag of carrots, but she wasn't going to tell him that and spoil the surprise.

"And for myself," she added, "a pair of jodhpurs, riding boots and a hard hat from the tack shop so I have the right clothes for when I exercise Pebbles. Aren't I lucky?"

Natty thought she saw Ned nod, although it might have been her imagination. He was still a picture in his pony poster until his amazing magic worked next time. Natty smiled, hoping that it would be soon.